This

DAVID BENNETT BOOK

belongs to

For my Mum and Dad

— Nicola Edwards.

First published in the United Kingdom in 2002
by David Bennett Books Limited,
64 Brewery Road, London N7 9NT.

A member of **Chrysalis** Books plc

This paperback edition first published in 2003.

BRITISH LIBRARY CATALOGUING-IN-PUBLICATION DATA
A catalogue record for this book is available from the British Library.

2 4 6 8 10 9 7 5 3 1

ISBN 1 85602 506 3
Printed in Singapore

Goodnight Baxter

by **Nicola Edwards**

DAVID BENNETT BOOKS

"Surprise!" said Daddy
as he opened his jacket
and out popped a puppy.

"I'm going to call him Baxter," said Charlie. Baxter licked Charlie's face.

Baxter and Charlie played all afternoon with the toys that Daddy had bought from the pet shop.

At bedtime, Charlie put Raster in his basket.

He gave Baxter
a goodnight kiss.
Then he went upstairs.

Baxter closed his eyes and tried to sleep...

in his basket...

on top of his basket...

under his basket...

over the side of his basket.

He even tried leaning
against his basket.
But it was no good.
He just couldn't sleep.

He had to go upstairs and find Charlie.

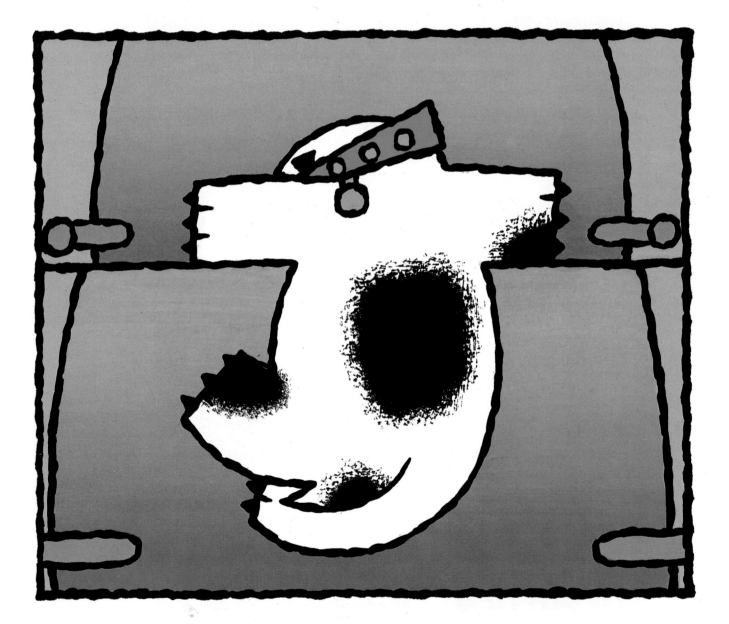

But every time Baxter tried to climb the stairs

he tumbled back down.

So he sat at the bottom of the stairs and barked.

Charlie tiptoed quietly downstairs with a warm, cosy blanket for Baxter.

But Baxter kicked it off...

jumped out of his basket...

and barked for Charlie.

So Charlie carried his favourite teddy bear downstairs for Baxter

But Baxter tossed it away...

jumped out of his basket...

and barked and barked for Charlie.

Charlie even found his old dummy and took it downstairs for Baxter.

But Baxter spat it out...

jumped out of his basket...

and barked and barked and barked
for Charlie.

But this time Charlie
didn't wake up.
He was fast asleep.

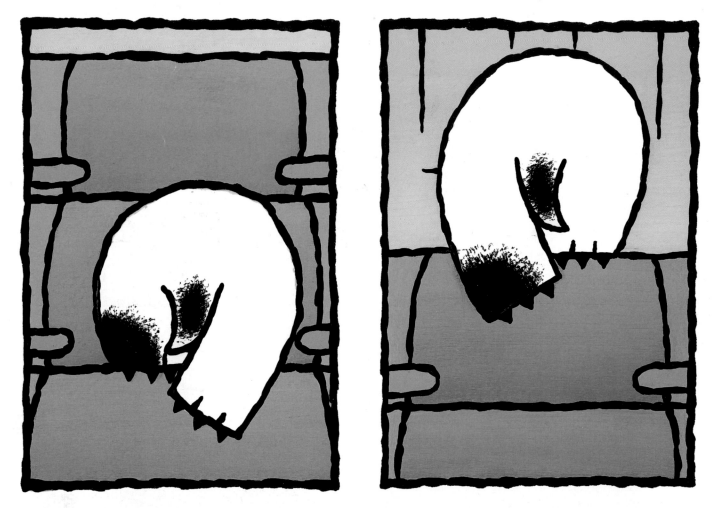

So Baxter wobbled and
stumbled up the stairs...
until he reached the top.

He pushed open Charlie's door with his nose.

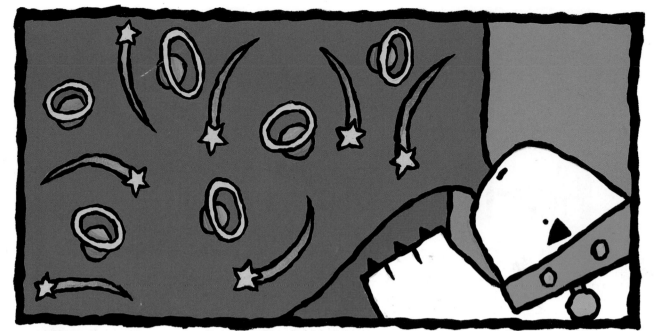

Baxter gave Charlie's blanket a little tug...

he put his wet nose on Charlie's hand...

he even licked one of
Charlie's ears... until
Charlie woke up.

Because Baxter didn't
want a blanket... or a
teddy or a dummy

He wanted Charlie!

"Goodnight, Baxter!"
said Charlie. And they
both fell fast asleep.

Also available from David Bennett Books

CLOSE YOUR EYES
Kate Banks
Illustrated by Georg Hallensleben

When a little tiger does not want to go to sleep, his mother
reminds him that just by closing his eyes he can enter a whole
new world of dreams and magical places.

Hardback ISBN 1 85602 457 1 £9.99

TRUFFLE GOES TO TOWN
Anna Currey

After the huge success of *Truffle's Christmas,* Truffle the mouse returns
in a brand new adventure, except this time he's off to town!

Hardback ISBN 1 85602 429 6 £9.99

MAX PAINTS THE HOUSE
Ken Wilson-Max

Max and his friends, Big Blue and Little Pink, all want to paint the house their
favourite colour. The only problem is that they all like different colours …

Hardback ISBN 1 85602 375 3 £9.99
Paperback ISBN 1 85602 502 0 £4.99

MAX'S STARRY NIGHT
Ken Wilson-Max

Max and his friends, Big Blue and Little Pink, all love to watch the stars. But Big
Blue is scared of the dark. How can Max help his big friend overcome his fear?

Hardback ISBN 1 85602 376 1 £9.99
Paperback ISBN 1 85602 412 1 £4.99

These books can be ordered direct from the publisher. Please contact the
Marketing Department, but try your bookshop first.